SUGAR, GUMMI, AND LOLLIPOP

THE PUPPY PLACE

**Don't miss any of these
other stories by Ellen Miles!**

THE PUPPY PLACE

SUGAR, GUMMI, AND LOLLIPOP

ELLEN MILES

SCHOLASTIC INC.

For everybody with a sweet tooth!

Text copyright © 2015 by Ellen Miles
Cover art by Tim O'Brien
Original cover design by Steve Scott

ISBN 978-0-545-85720-8

10 9 8 7 6 5 4 3 2 1   15 16 17 18 19

Printed in the U.S.A.   40

First printing 2016

CHAPTER ONE

Lizzie rolled down her car window and stuck her nose out for a good sniff. "I can smell the piney woods," she said. The air was fresh and clean.

"Just a little longer," Maria's mom said from the front seat. "Good thing, too. I bet Simba is about ready for a walk."

Lizzie turned in her seat to check on Simba, the big yellow Lab riding in the way-back. "Is that true, Simba?" she asked, giving him a scratch between the ears. Simba gave her a doggy grin and panted happily. As a guide dog (he belonged to Maria's mom, who was blind), he was not supposed to get petted while he was working. That meant he especially loved attention when he was "off duty." A long car ride definitely counted as off duty.

Lizzie Peterson had been to the Santiagos' weekend home in the woods a few times, and she loved it — even if it did take forever to get there. She loved the forest, the trails, and the sparkling lake. She loved the way they had to park way down below the cabin and haul all their stuff in red wagons, and she had even come to love how rustic it all was: no electricity or running water, the outhouse, the woodstove for heating. Most of all, she loved the cozy cabin and the sweet, tiny room she shared with Maria, her best friend. The only thing she didn't like was that she had to leave her darling puppy, Buddy, behind.

"You'll have Simba to spend time with," Mom had said when Lizzie begged to take Buddy along.

"And the rest of us would miss Buddy if he went away."

It was true. All the Petersons loved Buddy, the foster puppy who had come to stay. Lizzie's family took care of puppies who needed homes, usually just until they found each one the perfect forever family. She and her two younger brothers, Charles and the Bean, always had a hard time saying good-bye to the puppies they had helped care for. In Buddy's case, saying good-bye had been impossible. When it was time to find him a home, the whole family agreed that he belonged right there with them.

Lizzie closed her eyes, picturing Buddy's smooth brown coat and the heart-shaped white patch on his chest. He loved it when she scratched him there. She hoped Charles would remember to do that while she was gone. She sighed. Buddy would be fine. It was only a few days, after all.

Meanwhile, she and Maria would be having a fantastic time at the cabin. With luck, the lake might still be warm enough for swimming, and she and Maria planned to hike and climb trees and build fairy houses out of leaves and sticks and bark. Even though the cabin was in the middle of the woods, there was always plenty to do.

Lizzie's stomach rumbled. She needed a snack to give her energy for the hike to the cabin. She reached into the backpack at her feet and rummaged around until she found the candy bar she'd brought. "Want some?" she asked Maria as she peeled back the crinkly paper.

Maria's eyes widened. She held up her hands and shook her head. "Oh," she said. "I guess I forgot to tell you."

Mrs. Santiago swiveled around to face them. "Do I smell chocolate?" she asked.

"No, Mom," Maria answered quickly. "It's just —
nothing." She made a motion to Lizzie, pointing to
the backpack. "Put it away," she mouthed.

"Why? What's going on?" Lizzie asked.

"Didn't you tell her?" Maria's mother asked.

"I meant to," said Maria. "But —"

Mrs. Santiago shook her head. "Lizzie, we've
agreed that this is going to be a sugar-free weekend. Our family has been getting into the sweets
a little too much lately, and we decided we needed a
break."

Maria rolled her eyes and pointed at her mom.
"*She* decided," she said. "It sure wasn't my idea."

"Or mine," said Mr. Santiago from the driver's
seat. "But your mom does have a point. My cookie
eating was getting out of control."

"It's only a few days," said Mrs. Santiago. "I
think we'll survive."

Lizzie wasn't so sure. It wasn't as if her family ate sweets all the time. Her mom did not believe in junk food, and she was always very strict about how much of their Halloween candy they could eat each day. Still, they usually had something for dessert, even if it was just a cookie or two. It didn't seem fair that the Santiagos' rules had to apply to her.

She stared down at the chocolate bar in her hand. Then she sighed and pulled the wrapper back up to hide the delicious, melty sweetness. She tucked it into her backpack. "Okay," she said. She knew she was lucky to be asked to the cabin, and if this was the rule, this was the rule. She knew that was what her mom would say, along with "mind your manners" and "be a helpful guest." Anyway, maybe she'd be able to slip away and sneak the chocolate bar at some point. That would help her get through the sugar-free weekend. After all, she had never agreed to the idea in the first place.

"I'll take that," said Mrs. Santiago. "So you won't be tempted." She held out her hand.

Maria giggled. "She's on to you," she said.

"Just like my mom would be." Lizzie pulled out the chocolate bar again and handed it over. She still didn't think it was fair, but what choice did she have?

"Excellent," said Mrs. Santiago, tucking it into her purse. "You'll thank me, I promise. I bet we'll all feel so much better after even a few days without sugar. My friend Elaine says we'll probably lose the taste for it and never go back to our old ways."

"Elaine says a lot of things," muttered Mr. Santiago.

Maria's mom ignored him. She pulled a bag of nuts out of her own backpack and passed it around. "Almonds?" she asked. "Elaine says that nuts can help stave off a craving for sugar."

Everyone took a few, and by the time Lizzie had finished munching her handful, Mr. Santiago was pulling the car into a small clearing in the woods.

"Here we are!" He leaned back in his seat and stretched out his arms. "Time to unload."

Maria groaned. Lizzie knew that her friend was tired of all the packing and unpacking and lugging stuff around. The Santiagos went to the cabin almost every weekend. But Lizzie had plenty of energy. She couldn't wait to hit the trail, dragging a red wagon along the bumpy, rooty path. "It'll go quickly with all of us here," she told her friend. She jumped out and started to help Maria's dad load boxes and bags into the wagons that waited in a small shed at the side of the trail.

Soon they were ready to hike. Lizzie and Maria pulled one wagon while Mr. Santiago pulled the other. Simba, back at work in his harness now, led Mrs. Santiago and the rest of them up the well-worn path that wound through tall trees and over sparkling streams. Lizzie felt her excitement growing as they neared the end of the trail. She peered ahead, eager for her first view of the cabin. There it was, cute as ever, sitting in the middle of a small clearing. Soon smoke would be curling from the chimney, chili would be simmering on the stove, the cozy glow of gas lanterns would light the cabin, and their weekend would really get started. Lizzie knew that even without candy or cookies, she and Maria were going to have a blast.

"What's that on the porch?" She squinted toward the cabin.

"Looks like some sort of delivery," Mr. Santiago said. "A big cardboard box. Did you order something?" he asked his wife.

"Not me," she said. "But what's that sound?"

Lizzie strained to listen. "Something's crying," she said. "It sounds like —" She let go of the wagon handle and broke into a run, leaving Maria behind. She leapt up onto the cabin's porch and threw open the top flap of the box. "It is!" she shouted. "It's puppies!"

CHAPTER TWO

"No way!" Maria laughed out loud. "I know you must be kidding."

Lizzie stared into the box, then turned to look at her friend. She shook her head. "I'm not," she said. Then she bent down, reached into the box, and pulled out a small, wriggly brown puppy.

"Puppy!" Maria screeched. She galloped up to the cabin.

The puppy in Lizzie's hands shrank back and tried to climb inside her shirt. "Shhh," she said. "You're scaring it."

Maria slowed down as she moved closer. She climbed up the porch stairs and peered into the box. "Puppies," she whispered. "It really is pup-pies!" She reached in and pulled out another.

And another.

"Three of them!" Lizzie said after she'd checked the pink flannel blanket lining the inside of the box. She didn't want to miss any puppies. "I don't believe this."

"I don't, either," said Mr. Santiago as he joined them at the box. "What is a box of puppies doing on our porch?"

Mrs. Santiago shook her head as Simba led her up the porch steps. "Puppies?" she asked. "Really? I thought Lizzie was just fooling around."

"They're puppies, all right," said Lizzie. She stared down at the tiny, soft creature in her hands. "Hello, little guy," she said. "Where did you come from?"

The puppy stared back without blinking. Its eyes did not seem to focus perfectly, but it stuck out a teeny, tiny pink tongue and turned its head to lick Lizzie's thumb. A tingle went up her spine. "Oh!" she said. She bent to smell the top of the puppy's head. There was nothing like the smell of a very young puppy: it was sort of like sweet milk plus your favorite blanket plus maybe a spicy hint of nutmeg or cinnamon. She took a deep sniff. "Ahhh," she said.

Maria handed one of the puppies to her dad, and they all sat down on the porch to admire the dogs. "Sit, Simba," said Mrs. Santiago. "Now stay. Be a good boy." He sat very, very still, his nose twitching as he stared intently at the puppies. Mrs. Santiago sat next to her husband and put out a hand to touch the puppy he held. "So soft!" she gasped. "And" — she felt the puppy's head — "tiny! How old do you think they are? And tell me what they look like. I bet they're adorable!"

Lizzie held up her puppy to take a closer look. He filled both of her hands, but he didn't weigh more than a bag of chocolate-chip cookies. He was amazing. She wished Maria's mom could see him.

"They're light brown," she told Mrs. Santiago, "with short hair and little floppy ears. They have really beautiful black masks on their faces — oh, and their faces are all wrinkly! So cute." Her puppy had a black nose, big round eyes, and a funny curly tail. When he opened his mouth to yawn, Lizzie saw his tiny, sharp teeth. "I think they're really young," she said. "Like, they are probably just learning to eat solid food. I think this guy's baby teeth just finished coming in."

The puppy squirmed, and she pulled him back against her chest, where he seemed most comfortable. He probably felt safe there.

"Mine's a boy also," Maria said. "He's the cutest thing I ever saw." She sighed and kissed the top of her puppy's head, and the puppy nestled into her hands and licked her enthusiastically. Maria giggled. "I think he's a lovebug, too. He's not as shy as yours, Lizzie."

"Mine's a little girl, and she isn't shy at all!" Mr. Santiago said as his puppy struggled out of his arms and began to explore the porch, sniffing her way behind the big box. Mr. Santiago jumped up to catch her. "Hey, look what she found!" He handed the puppy to his wife, then went back to pick up a bag of puppy chow that had been hidden by the box. "I guess you're right about them being on solid food," he said to Lizzie. He scratched his head. "I just don't get it. Why would somebody leave puppies on our porch?"

"Dad, look," said Maria. "There's a note taped to the dog-food bag."

Her dad turned the bag around and pulled off a piece of lined notebook paper. "'We can't handle three puppies. Hope you can help,'" he read. He turned the paper over, then turned it back. "That's all it says." He scratched his head again. "What is going on here?"

"Somebody must know that we come up here every weekend," said Mrs. Santiago. "Maybe they've seen Simba, so they know we like dogs." She stroked the puppy's head, very gently. "Someone figured we would take care of them."

Lizzie was so shocked that she couldn't even speak. She felt a lump grow in her throat, and tears came to her eyes. Who would do such a thing? What if the Santiagos hadn't gone up to the cabin that weekend? The poor puppies could have starved — or frozen! And why would someone abandon three adorable, healthy puppies? They looked well fed, and they weren't dirty or crawling with fleas, the way some stray dogs were. Somebody must have left them there only hours earlier.

"Well, can we?" Maria asked.

"Can we what?" said Mrs. Santiago.

"Can we take care of them?" Maria lay her cheek along the puppy's head. "They need us!"

Lizzie felt her heart start to race. Three puppies to foster? Suddenly, the weekend was looking a lot more exciting. Who needed chocolate if you had puppies to play with? She held her breath, waiting to hear what Maria's parents would say. After all, she was just a guest.

"Well . . ." Mr. Santiago began.

"We can do it!" Lizzie couldn't help herself. "I've taken care of puppies this young before. I've even taken care of a younger puppy. Remember that cocker spaniel Bella? She had to be fed from a bottle. And I've taken care of more than one puppy at a time. Remember Chewy and Chica, the brother and sister Chihuahuas?" Lizzie had fostered so many puppies by then that she felt like a total professional. She could handle three puppies at once — no problem!

"I don't know," said Mr. Santiago. He held his chin in his hands as he stared at each of the puppies in turn. The one in Maria's arms was still licking her chin. Mrs. Santiago's puppy was struggling to get down and explore. And the timid little boy Lizzie held was nestled into her chest as if he was trying to hide. "Three puppies? It sounds like a lot of work. It's not exactly what I was planning on for this weekend." He sat down next to his wife. "What do you think?"

Maria's mom tilted her head. "Hmmm," she said.

CHAPTER THREE

Lizzie held her breath. She crossed her fingers — *and* her toes. Mrs. Santiago didn't say anything for what seemed like an hour — or maybe a year.

"To tell you the truth," she finally said, "I'm wondering if we really have any choice. It's too late to do anything about these guys today, especially since we don't really have phone service up here. Anyway, we need to get ourselves settled in the cabin before dark." She paused, and Lizzie wove her crossed fingers even tighter. "We'll have to keep them — at least overnight," she finally finished.

Maria let out a whoop, and the puppy in Lizzie's arms shrank against Lizzie's rib cage, almost as if he were trying to crawl right inside her. "Maria," said Lizzie in a low voice, "you really, really have to stop doing that."

Usually Maria hated it when Lizzie got bossy, but this time she just put a hand over her mouth. "Oops," she said. "I know. You're right."

Lizzie pulled her puppy in tight and wove her arms around him so that he was barely able to peep out. "It's okay," she whispered as she bent to kiss the velvety brown top of his tiny head. "Don't worry, little darling. We're going to take care of you — and the others."

Lizzie's heart pounded. Three puppies to foster — way out in the woods! This was something new. This was something fantastically wonderful. Suddenly, it took every bit of willpower she had to keep from shrieking just like Maria had. Instead, she kissed her puppy's head over and over, very softly and gently. He relaxed into her arms and fell asleep. She giggled. "When in doubt, take a nap," she said. "That's what Aunt Amanda says dogs think."

Lizzie felt a pang when she thought of her aunt. Aunt Amanda ran a doggy day-care center, and she knew pretty much everything about dogs, from how to give them baths, to what kinds of toys were best for which dogs, to how to train a dog to walk on its hind legs. How great would it be to have Aunt Amanda there now? Lizzie was supposed to be the puppy expert, but she knew she would have lots of questions — and Aunt Amanda could answer them. Not without cell service or a phone line, though. The cabin didn't even have electricity!

"So, what do we do first?" asked Maria.

Mrs. Santiago held up a hand. "If these little ones are staying, I think the first order of business should be for Simba to meet them. He's not supposed to play with other dogs unless I let him know it's okay, but I'm sure it's making him nuts to lie here watching me hold this little scamp." She gave Simba a command and a hand signal, and he got up from where he had been lying quietly beside her.

He reached up his neck to sniff the puppy who was now trying to struggle out of Mrs. Santiago's arms. His thick, feathered tail waved happily as he nuzzled the girl puppy back into place. She settled in with a sigh.

I was just trying to explore a little!

Then Simba walked over to Maria and let her puppy snuffle him all over his big, broad head. The puppy seemed to like Simba. He licked the big dog's nose with his tiny pink tongue.

Wow, you're a big guy. But I can tell that you're gentle. Are you going to help take care of us?

Finally, he approached Lizzie and waited patiently until the puppy in her arms peered out, curious about this big new creature. When Simba saw the puppy's twitching nose, he reached up his own to touch it gently. The puppy sniffed Simba carefully.

I guess I don't have to be too scared of you.

"Aww," said Lizzie. She felt her heart melt. "I think they're all going to get along just fine." She reached down to scratch Simba's head. "What a good boy," she told him.

Then everyone swung into action. They put the puppies back in the box — "Just for a few minutes, cutie!" Lizzie told hers as she lowered him in — and Mr. Santiago carried it inside. Then Mrs. Santiago put Lizzie and Maria to work unpacking the coolers as she bustled about, getting dinner started. Lizzie was always impressed by how easily Maria's mom moved around the cabin even though she couldn't see. She didn't need Simba's help at all in that small, well-organized space. It all had to do, Mrs. Santiago said, with making a sort of map inside her head so she could remember where everything was.

"I'll make a fire in the woodstove," said Mr. Santiago. "That will keep them cozy." He went out to the woodshed and came back with an armload of kindling and logs, then set to work.

Meanwhile, Maria and Lizzie rummaged through a blanket chest to find some old flannel sheets for a puppy bed. "Like a little nest," Lizzie said. "And maybe we should put some newspapers in one corner of the room. I mean, they're probably not house-trained yet. Ms. Dobbins says puppies need a place to 'do their business.'" Ms. Dobbins was the director of Caring Paws, the animal shelter where Lizzie volunteered.

"Maybe we should take them outside before we settle in," Maria suggested. "I hear them whimpering a little. Maybe they have some business to do right now."

"Great idea," said her dad. "I suggest that you take them one at a time, so you can keep track more easily."

Lizzie thought it couldn't be all that hard for two people to keep track of three puppies, but she didn't argue. She went to the box and lifted out the smallest puppy, the shy boy. "Ready for a pee?" she asked as she carried him to the door. Outside, she put him down on the ground. Instead of running off, he ran between her feet and huddled down as if he wanted to hide. "It's okay," she told him, picking him up gently and setting him in a patch of grass. "Go on, do your business."

The puppy plopped down on his butt and looked up at her.

It's kind of scary out here. Can't you just pick me up again?

Lizzie and Maria waited patiently until the puppy stood up, took a few unsteady steps, and finally squatted. "Good boy!" Lizzie said as she carefully scooped him up and brought him inside.

Next they took out the other boy puppy. All he wanted to do was lick and cuddle. When Maria put him down on the ground, he put his paws on Maria's knee and grinned up at her.

Come on, let's kiss some more!

When he finally did what they'd taken him out to do, Maria told him what a good boy he was. They brought him in and took the last puppy, the bold little girl, out of the box. "Your turn," said Lizzie. When she put her on the ground outside, the puppy scampered off toward the shed, then dashed toward the outhouse, then galloped over to check out the rain barrel, where the Santiagos collected water.

Whee! What fun to explore a new place!

"Hey!" said Lizzie as she and Maria chased after the little girl. "You wild child, you." She couldn't help laughing at the tiny explorer. After a few more minutes, the puppy squatted near the corner of the porch. Lizzie praised her, then scooped her up before she could take off again.

"Phew," Lizzie said as she carried the puppy inside. "This is going to be a lot of work. But at least they have the idea that they're supposed to be doing this out here, not inside."

"I wouldn't be so sure about that." Maria held her nose as she peered into the box. "I think we're going to have to wash this blanket."

Lizzie and Maria played with the puppies until dinnertime. It was so much fun to watch them toddle around on their unsteady legs. Their tiny tails stuck straight up as they explored the cabin, sniffing and pawing and licking — and peeing.

"Oops!" said Lizzie, scooping up the little girl puppy. "There she goes again." She ran the puppy outside, praised her when she squatted, and brought her back in. "This could be a problem," she said. "They're *really* not housetrained."

"Maybe we should think about building some sort of pen tomorrow," said Mr. Santiago, stroking his chin, "before they wreck the place. I think I have some scrap lumber in the shed."

After dinner, which they ate with puppies on their laps, Lizzie and Maria washed the dishes. After she'd dried the last bowl, Lizzie checked on the puppies. "Where's the little girl?" she asked. Mr. Santiago was holding one boy puppy while Mrs. Santiago stroked the other one.

"She was just under the couch," said Mr. Santiago. "I've been keeping an eye on her."

Lizzie looked under the couch. No puppy. She looked around the rest of the room. "I don't see her," she said.

"Could she have gotten into our bedroom?" asked Mrs. Santiago.

Lizzie went to check. "No!" she cried when she saw the girl puppy.

CHAPTER FOUR

The puppy was pawing through Mrs. Santiago's purse, which had been left next to the bed. Lizzie scooped up the pup and took her back into the main room. "She almost got into that chocolate," she said. "That could have been a real disaster. Chocolate can be poisonous for dogs." Lizzie sat down on the couch, feeling very tired all of a sudden. Maybe she wasn't the super puppy-fosterer she thought she was. Maybe this wasn't such a great idea after all.

Mr. Santiago sighed. "Maybe I'd better build that pen right now," he said, standing up and stretching. "They need a safe place to sleep, and that box is getting pretty stinky."

By bedtime, the pups were cozy in a wooden pen filled with blankets on one side and torn-up newspaper on the other. Still, nobody got much sleep that night: not Lizzie or Maria, who got up every couple of hours to check on the pups and take them out one at a time; not Mr. or Mrs. Santiago, who woke and grumbled every time the pups squealed; and not Simba, who kept whining as he tried to climb into the pups' new pen.

Finally, in the middle of the night, as Lizzie was putting the girl puppy back to bed, Mr. Santiago stumbled out of his bedroom, rubbing his eyes. He lit the gas lamp, grabbed his saw, and trimmed down one side of the pen so that Simba could step over it but the pups still could not. "There," he said to the anxious, pacing dog. "Is that what you wanted?"

In a moment, Simba leapt inside and settled into the blanket "nest." All three puppies snuggled right beside him and promptly fell asleep. "Aw," said Lizzie and Maria, who had watched the whole thing. After that it was easier to sleep, knowing that Simba and the puppies were safe and happy.

The next time Lizzie woke up, sunlight was streaming through the window. It was quiet outside the cabin; there was nothing but the sounds of birds singing and the breeze in the trees. But inside, the puppies made little yippy and growly noises as they tumbled and played inside their pen. Lizzie jumped out of bed and went to say good morning. The little girl pup was standing on top of both her brothers, reaching her paws nearly to the top of the box.

"Uh-uh-uh," Lizzie said. "I hope you don't grow too fast. You'll be able to climb out of here in no time." She lifted the bold little girl out of the pen. "How are you on this beautiful day? I think we need to give you and your brothers some names now that we're getting to know you."

Simba watched every move Lizzie made, as if he was making sure she was handling the puppy correctly.

"Don't forget, we won't have them for long," said Mrs. Santiago as she emerged from the bedroom. She pushed back the sleeves of her robe and went into the kitchen to get coffee started.

"I know," Lizzie said, getting up with the girl pup to take her outside. The little thing struggled in her arms and mouthed at her chin with tiny sharp teeth. "But Ms. Dobbins always says it's good to give puppies temporary names so you can start treating each one a little differently as you get to know their personalities. They need individual attention right now."

By then, Maria and Mr. Santiago were up. They each plucked a puppy out of the pen and met Lizzie at the door.

It was a beautiful morning, crisp and clear. The sky was blue and the air was fresh. Lizzie stood and watched, along with Maria and Mr. Santiago, as the puppies did what puppies need to do.

Mr. Santiago rubbed his eyes and yawned. "I'm ready for some coffee," he said. Then he frowned. "Coffee with no sugar," he added. "Ugh."

Maria and Lizzie exchanged smiles. Mr. Santiago had not been happy with their dessert the previous night, either. "Somehow an apple just doesn't satisfy my sweet tooth," he'd said, with a sad look at the piece of fruit in his hand.

"It's funny," Lizzie said now. "I don't miss sugar

as much as I thought I would. Maybe it's because these puppies are so sweet."

"That's it!" said Maria. She looked down at the shy little boy puppy who had run to hide between her feet. "We can give the puppies sweet names to match their personalities. Like, this one could be Gummi," she said.

Lizzie laughed. She knew Maria loved anything gummi: bears, worms, circles. Once Maria had heard that they had red frog gummis in Australia, and it was one of her big ambitions to eat one someday. "I like it," Lizzie said. "And I think this little girl should be . . . Lollipop! Because she's just so cute and bright and sweet." She laughed as Lollipop bit at her pajamas. Then she scooped the puppy up. "Ready for breakfast, Lollipop?"

Mr. Santiago knelt and opened his arms, and the other boy pup tumbled over himself as he ran to his new friend. "Come here, Sugar!" Mr. Santiago said. "This guy is just too lovable to have any other name."

"You're kidding!" was all Mrs. Santiago said when they told her the puppies' names back inside. Then she laughed and shrugged. "I should have known you'd all find a way to get around the no-sugar rule."

They put the puppies back into their pen. Lizzie and Maria washed their food and water bowls, filled them, and put them down. The puppies tumbled over one another in their rush for the food. "Oh, no!" said Maria. " Gummi isn't getting any."

"Gummi is an awfully funny name for a puppy," said Mrs. Santiago as she brought eggs and toast to the table for breakfast. Then she smiled. "But you know? I kind of like it."

Maria was busy helping the small, shy pup get enough to eat. "So do I," she said. "There you go, Gummi."

Lizzie and Maria gulped down their own breakfast while the puppies finished eating. Then it was time to take them outside again. Lizzie knew that puppies almost always had to "go" right after eating and right after waking up.

"I never knew puppies were so much work," said Maria.

"I know, it's crazy. But if we can get them started on their house-training, it will be much easier to find them homes," Lizzie said. She was tired of the routine, too. How did people take care of huge litters of puppies? She knew that sometimes mama dogs could have ten or twelve puppies at a time.

Maria borrowed her dad's phone and took picture after picture as the puppies roamed around the yard, stopping to sniff the grass or get into a wrestling match with each other. Their tiny squeaks went right to Lizzie's heart. "I wish I could keep them all," she said. "I also wish I knew what breed they are. It's hard to tell when they're this young, but those floppy ears and wrinkled faces are not going to change much. Neither are their adorable curly tails. I think they're puggles."

"Puggles?" Maria cracked up. "What a silly name. Where did that come from?"

Lizzie held up one hand. "Pug," she said. She held up the other. "Beagle." She grinned at Maria. "Get it?"

"So they're mutts?" Maria asked. "Mixed breeds, like Buddy?"

"Sort of," said Lizzie. "More like designer dogs, where somebody has bred two types on purpose. Like, how Labradoodles are a cross between a Lab and a poodle. Remember Gus? He was a Labradoodle." Gus had been one of most popular dogs the Petersons had ever fostered. Everybody wanted Gus, with his curly black hair and happy face.

Maria nodded. "I get it," she said.

"Puggles supposedly have the best qualities of both breeds," said Lizzie. "The beagle's longer nose means that they won't have some of the breathing problems that pugs can have — but they're friendly and sociable like pugs." She looked up as Mr. Santiago walked out of the cabin, car keys in hand.

"I'm off to the store for a few things," he said. "I'll pick up more puppy food and find out if anybody wants to adopt a puppy — or three." He reached out for his phone, and Maria handed it over.

"Can you e-mail some of those pictures to Ms. Dobbins and my aunt Amanda, too?" Lizzie asked. "Ask them if they think these pups are puggles. And maybe they'll have some tips on how to take care of them."

"Will do," said Mr. Santiago after Lizzie had told him the e-mail addresses. "Take good care of the pups while I'm gone." He headed down the path, and Lizzie had to chase after Lollipop to keep the adventurous pup from following him.

Maria checked her watch, then lay back on the grass and let all three puppies scramble over her. "It's only nine o'clock and I'm already tired," she said. "How are we ever going to keep these guys entertained all day?"

CHAPTER FIVE

Lizzie sat down next to Maria and pulled Lollipop into her lap. "When Buddy was little, we bought him all sorts of toys to keep him busy," she said as the little pup squirmed around and nibbled on her fingers. "Fluffy toys to cuddle with, chew toys to gnaw on, balls and Frisbees to chase. But it's not like there's a pet store anywhere near here."

"No way," Maria said. "Even if there was, we don't have any money."

"So we'll have to be creative." Lizzie jumped up, still holding Lollipop. "Let's go inside and see what we can find."

When the girls put the puppies back into their pen, Simba jumped in, too, and greeted them with sniffs and wags. He checked each one carefully, as if to make sure nothing had happened to them. Then he lay down and let the puppies snuggle up next to him.

"Awwww," said Maria. She led her mom to the pen and helped her feel around to "see" what Simba was doing. "Isn't that sweet?"

"Simba is full of surprises," said Mrs. Santiago. "Who knew he would be such a good mom?" She petted her dog's big head approvingly. "Good boy, sweetie," she said.

Lizzie and Maria went on a toy hunt through the cabin. "How about this, for a ball?" Lizzie showed her friend a rolled-up pair of socks she'd pulled from her backpack. "It's soft and won't hurt them. An older puppy might try to chew it up, but their baby teeth won't be strong enough to do that."

"Great," said Maria. "And when they do want to chew, how about this?" She held up the tube from an empty roll of paper towels.

"A woo-woo tube!" Lizzie said.

"A what?" Maria raised her eyebrows.

"That's what we call it in my family," Lizzie said. She took the tube from Maria. "Because you can do this." She put her mouth up to one end of the tube. "Woo-woo!" she called, as if through a megaphone. She did it very softly so she wouldn't scare the puppies.

Maria laughed. "That's the silliest thing I ever heard," she said.

Lizzie just shrugged. "Good toy, though," she said. "And with all the paper towels we're using for cleaning up messes, we'll have plenty of them."

When the pups woke from their morning nap, Lizzie and Maria were ready for them. After they took all three outside, they came back in and sat down to play with the homemade toys.

"Look! Sugar loves the rope!" Maria said. She had taken a length of rope and put several big knots in it. Now she played a gentle tug-of-war with Sugar while Lollipop scampered around, trying to catch an end of the rope.

Gummi was as shy as always, hiding behind Simba. Lizzie tried to tempt him with the sock ball, rolling it along the floor, but he shrank back from it. "I think he's freaked out by this thing that's moving by itself," Lizzie said. She tossed the ball for Simba to catch, and he snatched it easily out of the air. "See, Gummi? It's fun." She rolled the ball again, but Gummi just ran away from it and hid under a chair.

"Maybe he'd like the woo-woo tube," Maria said.

Lizzie took it from the kitchen table and brought it down to Gummi's level. Gently, she snaked it along the floor. "What's this?" she asked. "Ooh, looks like fun!"

Gummi put out a tentative paw.

What is this thing?

Lizzie pulled it back, teasing him a little. Then she moved it toward him. Gummi couldn't resist. He pounced and bit at the tube.

I'll get you!

Lizzie laughed. "Getting braver, little one!" she said.

By the time Mr. Santiago got home, the three pups were tuckered out and having their second nap of the morning (after another trip outside, of course). Lizzie and Maria lay at opposite ends of the couch, just waking from their own nap.

"I guess they really *aren't* any trouble, are they?" said Mr. Santiago when he saw the puppies sleeping in a cozy, warm pile in their pen.

Lizzie and Maria just laughed. "I think three puppies are about three hundred times more work than one," said Lizzie, rubbing her eyes.

"Guess what?" Mr. Santiago asked. "Ms. Dobbins agrees with you about their breed. She's pretty sure they're puggles!"

"Cool!" said Lizzie.

"Which is why nobody around here wants them, according to Mrs. Packer, the lady who runs the store." Mr. Santiago frowned down at the puppies.

"Why not?"

"Because most people around here use their dogs as hunting dogs. They are fine with beagles, who can find rabbits, but they're not interested in keeping a lapdog," said Mr. Santiago. "Mrs. Packer said that probably somebody's beagle met up with a summer person's pug — and nobody around here will want the puppies they made."

"So, if we haven't found them homes by the time we get back, will Ms. Dobbins take the puppies?" Mrs. Santiago asked.

Maria's dad shook his head. "She said in her e-mail that she's full to the brim and doesn't have room. I think we'll have to take them to the local shelter up here before we go. Either that, or your family will have to foster them," he said, turning to Lizzie with his eyebrows raised.

"We'll find them homes," Lizzie said. They had to. Of course she didn't want to take them to a shelter, but fostering was probably out of the question, too. She had to go back to school, for one thing. She was exhausted, for another. Even if she could talk Mom and Dad into fostering three puppies, she wasn't sure how much longer she could handle the work. "I promise we will! Look how adorable they are. How hard could it be?"

They all looked down at the puppies, nestled up together in their pen. Lizzie knew she had to be right. Sure, they were a lot of work — but who could resist these cuties?

CHAPTER SIX

"By the way, Lizzie," said Mr. Santiago, "your aunt Amanda wants to talk to you about the puppies. She e-mailed back right away."

"But how can I call her?" Lizzie asked. She knew that cell phones didn't work well near the cabin, and there was no regular telephone.

"I'll take you down to the store later this afternoon," said Maria's dad. "My phone gets pretty good service there."

Lizzie couldn't wait to tell her aunt all about the puppies. She knew Aunt Amanda would be envious, because Aunt Amanda loved pugs. In fact, she had three of them! She often said that pugs were sort of like potato chips — once you had one, it was hard not to have more.

Was Aunt Amanda interested in adopting one — or all — of the puppies? Lizzie's heart raced. That would be the best home ever for Sugar, Gummi, and Lollipop. But then she thought of her uncle James and knew it probably wouldn't happen. He loved dogs nearly as much as Aunt Amanda, but he definitely felt that they already had enough. Three pugs plus one big old golden retriever, Bowser, made a houseful.

Lizzie knew she would have to be patient and wait to find out what Aunt Amanda had to say. Mr. Santiago wouldn't want to race back to the store, since he always had four or five projects going at the cabin. He liked to spend his days puttering around in the woodshed, or hacking back brush in the woods near the outhouse, or creating a new trail to the lake. That was okay. She and Maria had things they wanted to do, too.

"Want to build fairy houses, like we planned?" Maria asked after lunch. "We can do it near the edge of the woods, and the puppies can play on the grass. Between the two of us, we should be able to keep track of them."

"Sounds great," said Lizzie. Maria had been telling her about fairy houses for a long time. Maria and her father had built them many times in the woods around the cabin, and Lizzie had seen pictures of them, but she'd never made one. She loved the idea of tiny houses in the woods made out of things you (or the fairies!) could find there.

They headed outside with the pups. Lollipop and Sugar tumbled over each other in their eagerness to gallop through the tall grass, but Gummi trotted along near Lizzie, almost tripping her as he wove between her legs.

When they got to the edge of the woods, by one of the trails that led to the lake, Lizzie was tempted to keep going. "Can't we just check out how the water looks?" she asked. She loved the secret little lake that glittered silver in the middle of the dark, piney woods — even though she'd once had a very scary experience there with a foster puppy she'd brought to the cabin, a Portuguese Water Dog named Baxter.

"We'd better not," said Maria. "At least, not with the puppies. What if one of them fell in? The water is pretty cold these days."

Lizzie knew her friend was right. It was late fall, and most of the leaves were already off the trees. The nights were chilly, and a mist lay over the ground early in the mornings. "Okay," she agreed as they headed back into the yard around the cabin. "So, what do we need for the fairy houses?"

Maria showed her how to gather twigs and pieces of pinkish-white birch bark. They scouted the forest edge for twisted roots, pretty pebbles, and tiny ferns that could be pulled up gently and replanted. Then, near the base of a huge old maple tree, they created a tiny village for tiny people: little thatch-roofed houses with ferns near the front door, a playground made from twigs stuck into the plush green moss that grew underneath, even a schoolhouse built from slabs of bark with a path of pebbles leading to the front entrance.

The puppies "helped" by grabbing every twig and piece of bark they could find and dragging it across the grass while Lizzie and Maria chased after them, laughing at their antics. Gummi had to be encouraged to play; Lizzie tossed bundles of dried moss for him to chase. He scrambled after them but then seemed terrified to pick one up, sniffing it and backing away.

What is that scary thing, anyway?

But Sugar and Lollipop were full of high spirits. Sugar tried to crawl into Maria's lap every time she sat down to place a twig or smooth some moss.

Hi! I love you!

Lollipop tried to squeeze into the schoolhouse and knocked the whole thing down. She plopped back onto her butt and stared up at Lizzie with innocent eyes.

Oops! I didn't meant to do it!

Between the puppies and the fairy houses, Lizzie barely noticed the afternoon fly by.

"Ready to go, Lizzie?" Mr. Santiago asked, wiping his hands on a greasy rag as he emerged from the toolshed. "I wouldn't mind a cup of coffee down at the store."

"Just don't put any sugar in it," Maria said, teasing her dad. "You're on the honor system, you know."

Her father smiled. "Cross my heart," he said. "No sugar in my coffee."

Maria borrowed his phone to take pictures of the fairy houses. "Before the puppies demolish them," she said.

Lizzie knelt to adjust a leaning fern and pat some bark into place. She loved the little town they had made, even if it wouldn't last. She wished she could live in a tiny wooden house with a soft green roof. How cozy it would be!

Mr. Santiago cleared his throat. "Ready?" he said again.

Lizzie stood up and brushed off her hands. "Ready," she said. After she had helped get the puppies back inside and kissed them each good-bye at least twice, Lizzie followed Mr. Santiago down the path to the car.

She watched the scenery as they drove to the store, noticing how much more "in the country" this place was than the area where her cousins lived. Here there were no big open fields or large houses. Instead, there were long driveways threaded up through the trees, with NO TRESPASSING signs at the ends of them, and small cabins with old trucks parked in front of them.

Lizzie had a feeling that people didn't have much money around here, and she wondered if that was why somebody had abandoned the puppies. Maybe they just couldn't afford to keep them.

When they stepped into the store, a big old tumbledown building with antique-looking gas tanks outside, Lizzie sniffed the air and let out a little moan. "Oh, that smells so good," she said. Her mouth watered.

"Another apple pie just came out of the oven. Got room for a third piece today?" asked the woman behind the counter.

Lizzie stared at her. A third piece? She hadn't even had one. Then she realized that the woman was looking at Mr. Santiago. Lizzie turned to look at him, too. He was blushing.

CHAPTER SEVEN

"Really?" Lizzie asked him. "Two pieces of pie?"

"With ice cream! I never saw anybody hoover up a plate of pie à la mode the way you did this morning," hooted the woman, who Lizzie realized must be Mrs. Packer. "You must have been pretty hungry."

Mr. Santiago looked at his feet. "I — well — I —"

"What about the honor system?" Lizzie put her hands on her hips and glared at him. "We're not supposed to be eating sugar this weekend."

"Uh-oh," said Mrs. Packer. "Me and my big mouth. Guess you're in trouble now!" She was grinning.

Mr. Santiago shrugged and held up his hands. "Guilty," he said. "I know it was wrong. I just couldn't resist when I smelled that pie."

Lizzie took another deep sniff. It really did smell delicious, all cinnamon-and-brown-sugary. It was hard to blame him.

"How about that phone call?" Mr. Santiago asked Lizzie. He was obviously in a rush to change the subject. He smiled at Mrs. Packer. "No more pie today, I guess. I'll just have a cup of coffee. No sugar." He pulled out his phone and handed it to Lizzie.

Lizzie just shook her head. She wondered if she should tell on him or let him get away with it. She hated to be a tattletale — and after all, it was only pie. On the other hand, he had agreed to the no-sugar weekend.

"The signal is a little better outside on the porch," said Mr. Santiago.

Lizzie looked down at the phone in her hand. "Okay," she said. "I'll be right back."

"You won't catch me eating pie, I promise," he said.

Lizzie pushed the door open and headed outside to sit in one of the rockers on the store's porch. She dialed Aunt Amanda's number.

"Hello?"

The connection was not very good. Lizzie wasn't even sure she had dialed the right number. "Aunt Amanda?" she asked.

"Lizzie? Is that you?"

"It's me," said Lizzie. "Mr. Santiago said you wanted me to call you."

"Plbst mrkel xningl puppies," said Aunt Amanda. At least that was what it sounded like. The connection wasn't getting any better.

"Yes, puppies!" said Lizzie. "We have three of

them. They're adorable! We named them Gummi, Sugar, and Lollipop."

"Bungee?" Aunt Amanda asked. "Booger? Malaprop?"

Lizzie smiled. Close enough. "I wish you were here to give us advice," she said.

"Gargle bigstrom," said Aunt Amanda. "Quiggle vox m-boy?"

"Two boys," said Lizzie, hoping that was what her aunt was asking. "Two boys and a girl."

"Gourd," said Aunt Amanda. "I glite mach schones."

Lizzie rolled her eyes. This was ridiculous. She really couldn't understand a word Aunt Amanda was saying. "I think they're only about six weeks old," she said, in case her aunt could hear her better than she could hear her aunt. "And Ms. Dobbins agrees with me that they are probably puggles. I don't think we'll find any homes for them around here, so I'm hoping to bring them back to Littleton with us."

"Glitch."

That was the last word Aunt Amanda said before the call was dropped. Lizzie looked at the phone. There was only one dot, which on her mom's phone meant hardly any signal. It wasn't worth trying again, at least not right then. She went back inside and handed the phone to Mr. Santiago, who sat sipping a mug of coffee. There was no evidence of pie.

"Did she have any ideas?" he asked.

Lizzie shook her head. "If she did, I couldn't hear them. The phone wasn't working so well."

"The connection goes up and down all the time around here," said Mrs. Packer. "Depends on the time of day, the weather, and probably the position of the stars and planets or something. Try again, you might get a better signal."

"Maybe tomorrow," said Lizzie. She was eager to get back to the puppies.

On the way home, Mr. Santiago turned to Lizzie with an embarrassed smile. "So, are you going to tell on me?" he asked.

"Depends," said Lizzie, crossing her arms.

"On what?" he asked.

"On whether you stop talking about taking those puppies to the local shelter," she said. "They need really good homes, and it sounds like we're not going to find them around here."

Mr. Santiago nodded. "Fair enough," he said. "I'm beginning to see that it makes sense to bring them back to Littleton with us, anyway. And for my part, I promise not to sneak any more sugar."

"Deal," said Lizzie as he pulled the car into the cabin's parking spot. She jumped out and started up the trail. She couldn't wait to see Lollipop, Sugar, and Gummi. She ran ahead of Mr. Santiago, leaping over roots and rocks as she galloped up the trail. But when she got to the cabin, she saw Maria sitting on the steps, crying.

She rushed to her friend. "What's the matter?" she asked.

Maria choked back a sob. "Lollipop is missing," she said.

CHAPTER EIGHT

"Missing? What are you talking about?" Lizzie sat down next to Maria and put her arm around her friend.

"Lollipop disappeared! I've looked everywhere, and I can't find her." Maria wiped her nose on her sleeve.

"How could that have happened?" Lizzie asked. "Weren't you watching them?"

Maria broke into loud sobs. "I was! I was! I knew you'd think it was my fault. But I promise, I never took my eyes off them. We were inside the whole time, except for when I took them out to pee, one at a time."

"I don't think it's your fault." Lizzie patted Maria's back. "Of course I don't. But where could she have gone?"

"That's what I can't figure out. Even Simba can't find her, and he has nosed around every inch of the cabin. He knows something's wrong. And the other two puppies won't stop crying. I think they miss their sister." Maria put her head down and wailed.

"Honey! What is it?" Mr. Santiago, who had lagged way behind Lizzie on the path, emerged from the woods. "Are you all right?" He ran to the porch and put his arms around Maria. "What is it? Is Mom okay?"

"We're fine," gasped Maria through her sobs. "But Lollipop is gone."

"Gone? Where?" Mr. Santiago looked as shocked as Lizzie felt.

"I don't know!" Maria wailed. "That's what I'm trying to tell you!"

"Okay, okay." Mr. Santiago hugged Maria closer. "Easy, now. Let's go inside and talk this over calmly. She's just a little puppy. How hard can it be to find her?" He helped Maria to her feet and led her into the cabin. Lizzie followed, feeling a knot in her stomach. This wasn't good. This wasn't good at all.

Inside, the two boy puppies were crying, just as Maria had said. Their little yips and wails broke Lizzie's heart. They sat in their pen, huddled together for comfort. She went straight over to them and lifted them both out, hugging them to her chest. "Shhh, shhh," she said, kissing the tops of their sweet-smelling heads.

Simba paced back and forth, sniffing the floor, the couch, the wood box near the stove, the kitchen cabinets.

Mrs. Santiago was bent over a trunk, rummaging through blankets and pillows. She turned when she heard them walk in. "I thought she might have gotten stuck inside this somehow. But there's definitely no puppy in here." She stood up and put her hands on her head. "Think!" she said. "If I were a puppy, where would I go?"

"Are you sure she's inside?" Mr. Santiago asked. "The door wasn't open at any point, was it?"

Maria shook her head. "No way," she said. "No. Like I said, I took them each out, one at a time, but I would never leave the door open, even with them in their pen." She started to cry again. "Why does everybody think it's my fault?"

"I wasn't accusing you," said her dad. "Just asking. Let's all calm down and try to be logical." He thought for a moment, stroking his chin. "How about if we each take a room and search as carefully as we can? Under beds, inside drawers, behind furniture."

"We did that already," said Maria. "Mom and I did that."

"Let's do it again, just to be sure." Her father moved toward the front of the cabin. "I'll do the kitchen," he said.

Lizzie nestled the two puppies back into their pen, then patted the blanket and called to Simba. "Come on," she said. "Keep them company. They need you."

The big dog hesitated and nosed Mrs. Santiago's hand as if to ask if it was all right. She urged him on with a pat on the head. "She's right, Simba. Take care of those little boys."

Simba climbed into the pen and settled himself next to the puppies. They snuggled in close and stopped crying almost immediately. "Good dogs," said Lizzie. She stood up and dusted off her hands. "I'll check our bedroom."

"I'll do Mom and Dad's," said Maria.

"And I'll do the living room. There aren't too many hiding places, and I can feel them all," said

Mrs. Santiago. She walked to the couch and pulled the cushions off it, patting around under each one.

Lizzie took a quick look around the bedroom she shared with Maria. Then she started at one side and checked every inch of the room until she got to the other side. She lifted up bed pillows and pulled off the quilts. She looked under the beds. She opened the little closet where the Santiagos stored extra clothes for cold weather. She poked through her backpack and Maria's. She opened the drawers on the nightstands that stood next to the twin beds, even though they were too small to hide even a tiny puppy like Lollipop.

No puppy.

"No puppy," said Mr. Santiago as he walked out of the kitchen.

"No puppy," said Maria and Mrs. Santiago. Maria sat down heavily on the couch and began to cry again, quietly this time. Her mom sat down next to her and patted her arm.

"Think! Think!" Mrs. Santiago said to herself again. She tilted her face to the ceiling. The room was so quiet that Lizzie could hear the fire in the woodstove crackling and popping. Suddenly, Mrs. Santiago stood up, a hand to her mouth. "Maybe the door *was* open," she said. "Just for a minute, when Simba and I went out to get more wood for the fire."

"I was outside with Gummi then," said Maria. "I saw you go to the woodshed." She stood up, too.

"And the other puppies were in their pen. I thought it was safe." Mrs. Santiago's face had turned white. "If Lollipop managed to get out of the pen — and then get out of the cabin . . ." She shook her head. "She could be anywhere!"

CHAPTER NINE

They all stared at one another. "What do we do?" Maria asked. Lizzie could see that her friend's lip was trembling, but Maria had her fists clenched and a determined look on her face. She was obviously trying hard to hold back more tears. "We need a plan."

"Take Simba outside," said Mrs. Santiago. "I'll stay with the puppies. He'll know where to look."

"Good idea," said Mr. Santiago. "Let's go, girls." He clicked his tongue and called to Simba. "C'mon, big boy. We've got a job to do."

Simba didn't move. He seemed to feel as if he

already had a job to do: taking care of the two puppies who were left.

"Mom, tell him it's okay," said Maria.

Mrs. Santiago went to the puppy pen and reached in to put a hand on Simba's head. "It's okay, sweetie," she said. "I'll be here with these guys. You go ahead and find their sister."

Simba got to his feet. Gummi and Sugar started to cry again, but Mrs. Santiago scooped them up and soothed them. "It's okay, little ones," she said.

Simba gave the puppies one last worried look, then turned to follow Mr. Santiago and the girls outside.

"Where's Lollipop?" Lizzie asked Simba, the same way she would ask Buddy where his favorite toy was. Buddy was always great at finding Mr. Duck or his spongy football when she asked that. He would race around, sniffing wildly, until he pounced, grabbed it, and pranced back to her proudly to show off his prize.

Simba stood on the porch with his nose in the air, sniffing. Lizzie saw his nostrils working as he sorted out all the scents that surrounded the cabin. She knew that his nose — any dog's nose — worked about ten thousand times better than her own. She could smell pine trees, and the musty scent of wet leaves on the ground, and maybe a whiff of the lake. Simba, on the other hand, could probably smell a coyote den three miles away, or a rabbit hopping through the forest, or even the scent of the person who had left that box full of puppies on the porch.

Lizzie shuddered at the thought of coyotes. She had heard them howling at night sometimes, during other visits. Lollipop would make a perfect snack for a hungry coyote.

"Where is she, Simba?" Lizzie asked again. "Find her. Find Lollipop."

Simba looked up at her. Then he sniffed some more. He leapt off the porch and put his nose to the ground, snuffling harder. He ran back and forth across the grass in front of the porch, sniffing and snuffling. He stopped at one point and held his head up high, as if he was listening, then put his nose to the ground again.

Suddenly, his tail began to wag. He sniffed — sniffed harder — then began to run in a straight line.

"I think he's got the scent!" said Mr. Santiago. "Follow him!"

Lizzie and Maria jumped off the porch and ran after Simba. With his nose still to the ground, he dashed behind the cabin and straight toward the woodshed.

"Oh," said Mr. Santiago, who had also come running. "Maybe not. He's probably just following your mom's track."

Simba went to the woodshed door and began to bark. He lifted a paw and scratched at the door. He barked some more. Scratched some more.

Then, in a moment of silence, Lizzie heard it: a tiny whimper from inside the shed. "She's in there!" she shouted as she ran to open the door.

Sure enough, the minute the door swung open, Lollipop tumbled out. She shook off, and wood chips went flying. She leapt at Simba with a happy little puppy bark.

Boy, am I glad to see you, old pal!

Simba sniffed her, and his tail wagged mightily. Lizzie scooped her up. "You naughty girl!" she said as she hugged the tiny pup close. "You had us so worried."

Lollipop snuffled at Lizzie's cheek and gave her chin a little nibble.

What's the problem? I'm fine. It was just a little adventure.

Maria wiped tears from her eyes and reached out. "Give me a turn with that scamp," she said. Lizzie handed her over, and Maria nuzzled the puppy's head with her cheek.

"What a good boy, Simba." Mr. Santiago petted the big dog. He rumpled Simba's ears and bent down to kiss his head. "What a hero. Let's go inside and get you a really good treat."

"And let's take *you* inside for a big reunion with your brothers," Maria said to Lollipop.

"Or better yet, I'll go get them," said Lizzie. "I'm sure they're ready for a chance to come outside. I can't wait to tell your mom that we found Lollipop."

She ran inside and told Mrs. Santiago the good news. Maria's mom burst out crying when she heard. "What a relief!" she said. "I would never have forgiven myself if something happened to that sweet little puppy."

"It wasn't your fault," said Lizzie. "Who knew that Lollipop had figured out how to climb out of the pen?" She reached in for the other two puppies and held them to her chest. "You're in for a happy surprise," she told them. She headed back outside and put them on the grass near Lollipop.

The three puppies ran toward each other with tiny squeals of joy.

Sugar pawed at Lollipop's nose.

There you are!

Gummi rolled over and licked her chin.

We missed you!

Lollipop pounced on top of both of them.

Yay! I missed you, too!

Lizzie and Maria laughed — with tears in their eyes — as they watched the puppies tumble and play. "How will we ever split them up?" Lizzie asked. "Wouldn't it be cool if we could find somebody who would take all three?" She knew it wasn't likely, but still.

"That's not going to be easy," said Maria. "Who has room for three dogs?"

Just then, a voice rang out from the path through the woods. "Yoo-hoo, anybody here?"

CHAPTER TEN

"Boy, Mrs. Packer wasn't kidding when she said your place was back of beyond," said a red-faced woman, huffing and puffing from her trek up the trail. She stuck out a hand as she approached. "Gloria," she said. "Came about the free puppies."

Lizzie and Maria exchanged glances, then stood up and shook hands with the stranger. "Did Mrs. Packer tell you about them?"

"That's right. I'm the one who makes the pies. I just delivered some fresh ones — blueberry — and she told me you had some pups to get rid of. She said you don't have a phone up here, so I figured I'd just come on up." She looked down at the puppies. "Well, they're just little things, aren't they?"

"Pies?" asked Maria.

"They're probably only about seven weeks old," Lizzie said in a hurry, before Gloria could say more. "But they all have their own personalities already." Lizzie rattled on, telling Gloria about each of the puppies.

She noticed that Gloria hadn't said "cute little things" or "adorable little things." Nor did she bend down to greet the puppies. She just stood there looking at them, as if she was trying to figure out what they were good for. Right away, Lizzie felt a tingle in her spine that told her that while Gloria might be a very good pie maker, she was not the right person for these pups. They needed love, and lots of it, after being taken away from their mother so early. Still, the puppies did need homes. Maybe she should give Gloria a chance. Anyway, she didn't want to be rude.

She squatted down and picked up Sugar and Lollipop. Maria scooped up Gummi. "Are you interested in adopting one of them?" Lizzie asked.

"Oh, we'll take all three, I guess," Gloria said. "Stan — that's my husband — wants to try to raise 'em up for hunting rabbits. They *are* part beagle, right?" She squinted down at the pups. "They sure don't look it."

"Well, we think they are," Lizzie said carefully. "But we're not promising anything. They just showed up on our porch."

"So I heard," Gloria said. "So you don't really have any claim on them, exactly."

"Well . . . ," began Lizzie. She looked at the cabin, wishing that Mr. and Mrs. Santiago would come out.

Maria seemed to read her mind. "I'll go get

Mom and Dad," she said. She handed Gummi to Lizzie and headed inside.

"So, your husband knows how to train dogs?" Lizzie asked. Three squirming puppies in her arms was tough to handle. She put Gummi and Sugar back down on the ground, but held on tightly to Lollipop.

"He tries," sighed Gloria. "So far he hasn't had much luck. I swear, he's put enough money into that fancy outdoor pen and shock collars and everything. You'd think he'd have a few rabbit skins to show for it, but so far his dogs have been duds. He's hoping for better with these."

Lizzie closed her eyes. Pen? Shock collars? "So the dogs would live outside?" she asked. She knew that plenty of people who used dogs for hunting kept them outside in big pens with high wire fences. If they were warm enough, and had enough food and water, it could be all right — but she

hated to think of these sweet little puppies spending their lives in a plywood house with straw for
their bedding. And shock collars? She was not
into that idea — not at all.

"Plus," Gloria went on, "if it doesn't work
out, we can always sell them. My cousin says
city people pay big money for these so-called
designer dogs."

Lizzie wondered about that, too. Would Gloria
and her husband make sure that the pups went
to good homes? "Um, I don't know if —" she
began, but just then, the cabin door swung open.

"Hello there!" Mr. Santiago came out of the
cabin and walked over to shake hands with
Gloria. "I hear you're interested in the puppies?"

"That's right," said Gloria. "But this little girl
doesn't seem so ready to let them go." She let out
a fake-sounding jolly laugh.

"Well," said Mrs. Santiago, who had also come

outside, "it's important to us that these puppies go to good homes."

"Are you saying my home isn't good enough?" Gloria put her hands on her hips. "I guess at least one of you thought my pies were worth eating."

"No, no, no!" Mr. Santiago blushed deep red as he held up his hands. "It's not that —"

"Helloooo!" someone called from the edge of the trail. Lizzie turned — and smiled.

"Aunt Amanda!" she said.

"In the flesh." Aunt Amanda smiled back at her. "I got here as quickly as I could. You haven't given any of those puppies away yet, have you?" She walked straight over to Gummi and Sugar and knelt down to let them climb all over her before she even came over to hug Lizzie and take Lollipop from her arms.

Lizzie glanced at Gloria. "Well, no," she said. "Not yet."

"Good, because I had first dibs, right? I know you couldn't hear everything I was saying with that terrible phone connection, but I hope you understood that much." Aunt Amanda sat down on the ground with all three puppies and giggled as Sugar nibbled at her earlobe, Lollipop tried to jump onto her head, and Gummi let himself be scratched between the ears. "My friend Susie does puggle rescue, and she's got a whole list of people waiting for puppies. She's checked them all out and they're all wonderful owners who are dying to give a puppy a forever home."

Lizzie smiled. "Really? That's fantastic." Three happy homes would be much better than being together in an outdoor pen, wearing shock collars. She glanced at Gloria, shrugged, and held up her hands. "Sorry," she said. "I guess they're not available after all."

For a second, Gloria looked like she was about

to say something, maybe something angry. Then she shrugged, too. "Oh, well," she said. "I sure wasn't looking forward to spending all that money on dog food, anyway. Stan will just have to keep looking for some dogs to train." She nodded, turned, and started to leave. "Thanks anyway," she called over her shoulder as she headed down the trail. "And don't forget: I just dropped off some pies at the store. If you liked the apple, you'll love the blueberry."

As she disappeared, Lizzie let out a long breath. "Phew," she said to Aunt Amanda. "You got here just in time."

"Good thing," said Aunt Amanda. Now she held Sugar in her arms, nuzzling his little head. "I can see right away that these puppies are in terrific shape. You've done a great job taking care of them."

Lizzie plopped down on the ground next to her aunt and pulled Lollipop onto her lap. Maria sat down, too, and picked up Gummi. They grinned at each other. "Thanks, Aunt Amanda," said Lizzie. Maybe she was a super fosterer after all — as long as she had help. "It was a lot of work, but we all pitched in."

"I think this calls for a celebration," said Mrs. Santiago. "Our sugar-free weekend can wait for another time. Ever since I heard the word 'pie,' I'm having this incredible craving for a big slice." She gave her husband a teasing look. "Somehow I have a feeling you might know where to find some."

"Um," said Mr. Santiago. He looked at Lizzie, but she just held up her hands as if to say 'I didn't tell.' He looked back at Mrs. Santiago and nodded. "Sure, I think I can round up some pie — and maybe some ice cream to go with it?" He reached into his pocket and pulled out the car keys. "I'll be back in a jiffy," he said.

Lizzie and Maria sat outside with Aunt Amanda, telling her all about the puppies, as the sun set and the sky grew dark. By the time the first twinkling star came out, Lizzie was ready with her wish. "May these puppies have happy lives, in safe and loving homes," she said, looking up at the sky as she pulled Lollipop close. "May *all* puppies everywhere have that. That's my only wish."

Aunt Amanda put an arm around her and kissed the top of her head. "That's a wonderful wish," she said. "I hope it comes true."

"Me too," said Maria. Then she laughed. "And I think *my* wish is coming true right now." She pointed to the beam of a flashlight bobbing through the woods. "Here comes Dad with the pie!"

PUPPY TIPS

Young puppies need special care and plenty of attention. If it seems like the puppies in this book had to go outside and "do their business" a lot, that's because it's what young puppies do! They also sleep a lot, and wrestle with each other, and chew on everything as they try to learn about their new world. If you don't have a chance to be around real puppies, ask a parent or teacher to help you find a "puppy cam" online, where you can watch a litter of puppies grow up. It's a lot of fun!

Dear Reader,

Ever since I wrote CHEWY AND CHICA I have thought it would be fun to write another book about more than one puppy — and I have always wanted to write about cute, mischievous puggles. At first I thought the book would be about two puppies, but then I thought — "How about three?!" — and that was that. (One of the best things about being an author is that you get to make the story any way you want it.) As for their names — well, I have to admit that just like Mr. Santiago, I have a sweet tooth! I hope you've enjoyed reading about Sugar, Gummi, and Lollipop as much as I enjoyed writing about them.

Yours from the Puppy Place,
Ellen Miles

P.S. For another book with more than one puppy, check out BUDDY. Then there's MAGGIE AND MAX, which features a puppy — and a kitten!

ABOUT THE AUTHOR

Ellen Miles loves dogs, which is why she has a great time writing the Puppy Place books. And guess what? She loves cats, too! (In fact, her very first pet was a beautiful tortoiseshell cat named Jenny.) That's why she came up with the Kitty Corner series. Ellen lives in Vermont and loves to be outdoors with her dog Zipper every day, walking, biking, skiing, or swimming, depending on the season. She also loves to read, cook, explore her beautiful state, play with dogs, and hang out with friends and family.

Visit Ellen at www.ellenmiles.net.